Dear Jack,
Happy Birthday
to a Brillant
Boy !! :)

We Love you!
Mr. + Mrs. Grennan
Molly + Sean

# THE
# Tower to the Sun

## COLIN THOMPSON

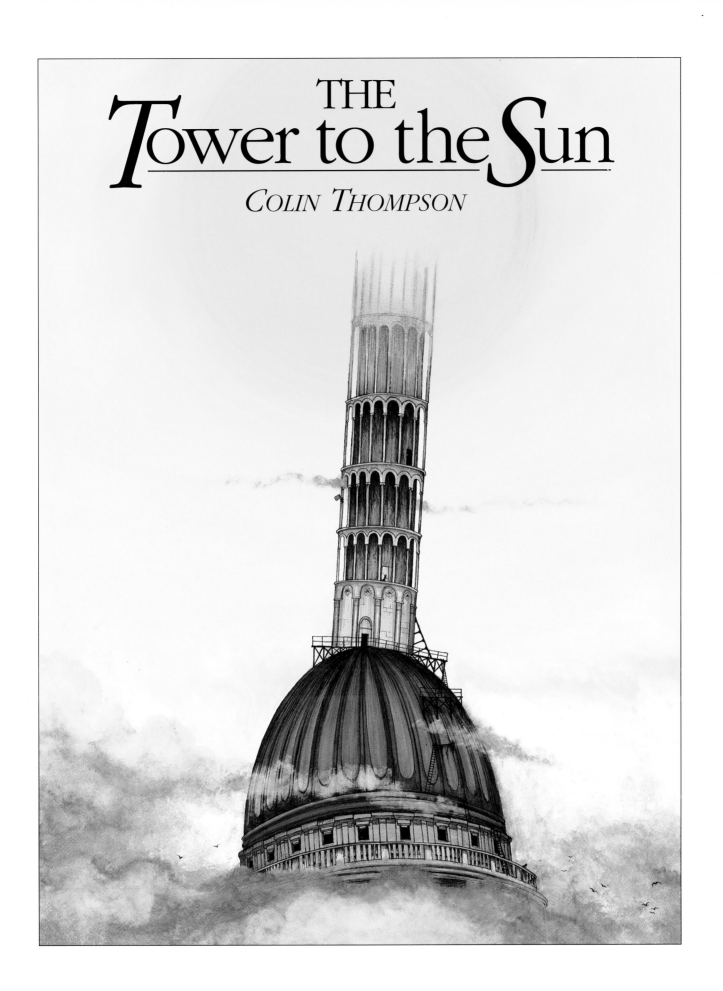

*Alfred A. Knopf* ❧ *New York*

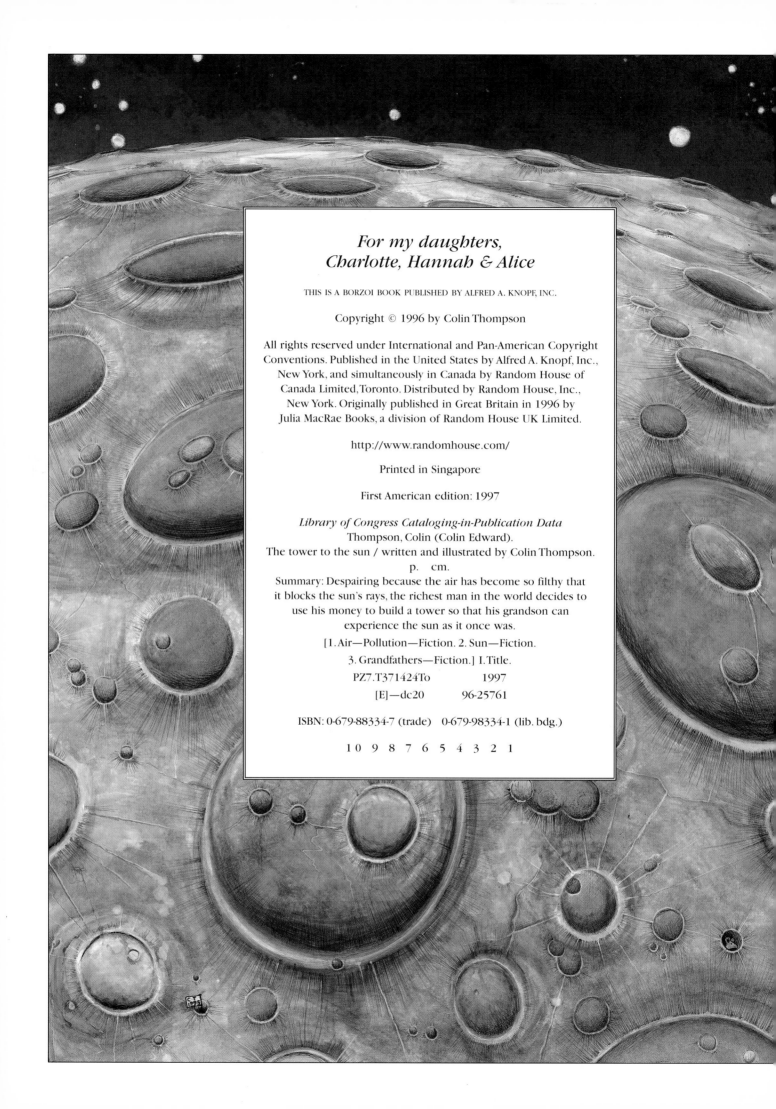

*For my daughters,*
*Charlotte, Hannah & Alice*

THIS IS A BORZOI BOOK PUBLISHED BY ALFRED A. KNOPF, INC.

Copyright © 1996 by Colin Thompson

All rights reserved under International and Pan-American Copyright
Conventions. Published in the United States by Alfred A. Knopf, Inc.,
New York, and simultaneously in Canada by Random House of
Canada Limited, Toronto. Distributed by Random House, Inc.,
New York. Originally published in Great Britain in 1996 by
Julia MacRae Books, a division of Random House UK Limited.

http://www.randomhouse.com/

Printed in Singapore

First American edition: 1997

*Library of Congress Cataloging-in-Publication Data*
Thompson, Colin (Colin Edward).
The tower to the sun / written and illustrated by Colin Thompson.
p.   cm.
Summary: Despairing because the air has become so filthy that
it blocks the sun's rays, the richest man in the world decides to
use his money to build a tower so that his grandson can
experience the sun as it once was.
[1. Air—Pollution—Fiction. 2. Sun—Fiction.
3. Grandfathers—Fiction.] I. Title.
PZ7.T371424To            1997
[E]—dc20            96-25761

ISBN: 0-679-88334-7 (trade)    0-679-98334-1 (lib. bdg.)

10  9  8  7  6  5  4  3  2  1

Once upon a time, if you stood on the moon and looked down at the earth, you could see the Great Wall of China. Winding over sharp mountains and through deep valleys, it lay on the earth like a great sleeping snake. From space it was the only sign of human existence. For over two thousand years it had shown people on distant worlds that they were not alone.

A hundred years later, looking back at the earth through the empty sky, you could see nothing but clouds. From side to side, the oceans, the land, and the Great Wall all lay beneath a never-ending mask of yellow mist. Like a pale copy of the sun, soft and blurred at the edges, the tired planet sat alone in the vastness of space.

The richest man in the world looked out across the city and said to his grandson, "When I was your age, the sky was blue and the sun was so bright that you couldn't look at it."

"I know," said the boy. "I've seen pictures."

"I wonder if it's still blue," the man said, "up there above the clouds."

There was no way they would ever know. There was so little fuel left on earth that it was needed for more important things than journeys through the clouds.

"The world was so big," said the man. "You could stand on top of a mountain and see for hundreds of miles. You could see tiny streams grow into great rivers and roll across a dozen countries until they finally grew into endless oceans."

The boy looked into the gloom and said nothing. The dull fog was all he had ever known.

"It's all so small now," said the old man. "You can't even see the mountains. The sky sits on our shoulders."

The dark sky grew darker and they knew it was night.

The richest man in the world looked out across the city. It was winter and tired snow covered everything. The sky hung dark above the earth all day like an old blanket. But unlike a blanket, it brought no warmth to the world. Only the weakest wash of sunshine came through and all the heat was on the outside. The old man shivered in his thick coat and said, "I'd give anything to see the sun once more."

"Couldn't we fly through the clouds?" said his grandson. But planes didn't fly anymore, not even for the richest man in the world.

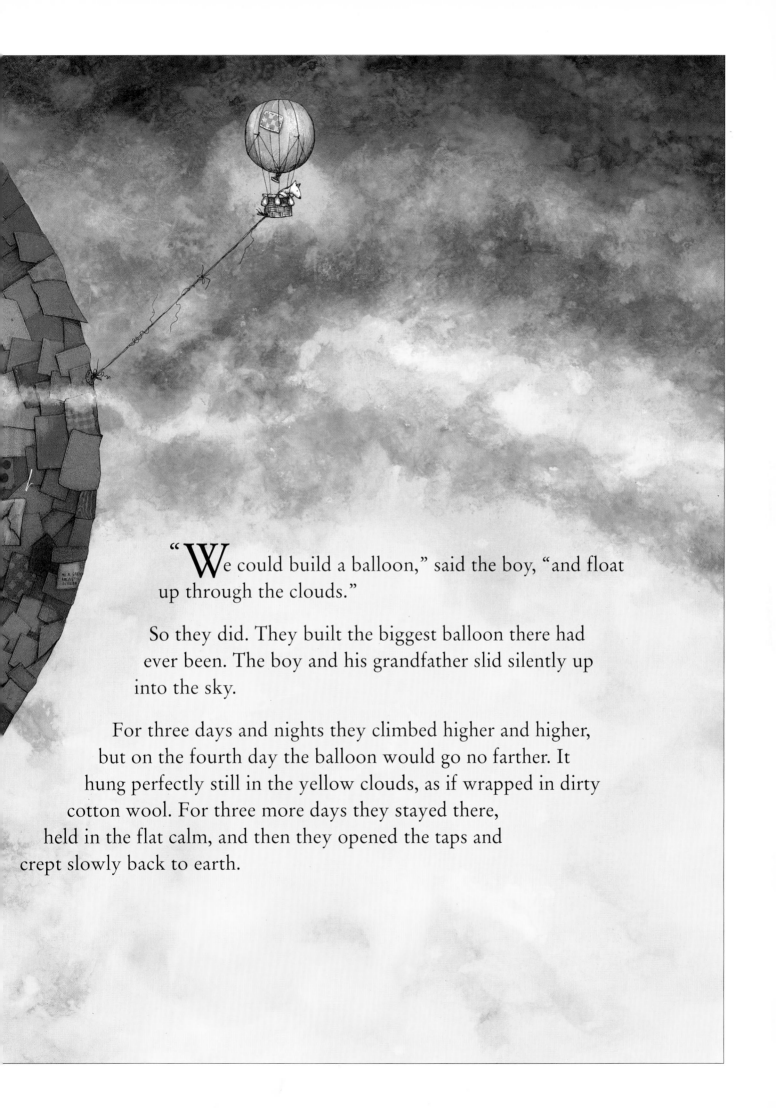

"We could build a balloon," said the boy, "and float up through the clouds."

So they did. They built the biggest balloon there had ever been. The boy and his grandfather slid silently up into the sky.

For three days and nights they climbed higher and higher, but on the fourth day the balloon would go no farther. It hung perfectly still in the yellow clouds, as if wrapped in dirty cotton wool. For three more days they stayed there, held in the flat calm, and then they opened the taps and crept slowly back to earth.

"We could build a tower," said the boy. "A tower to the sun."
The old man was about to say that it would be impossible. A tower tall

enough to break through the clouds would never stand up. But he thought,
Why not? What use is all my money if I can't build dreams?

Far away from all the cities and towns, on the biggest rock in the world,

ten thousand people began to build a city to the sky.

For ten years they worked. The richest man
in the world grew older and his grandson
became a man.

For twenty years they worked. The richest man in the world grew very old and his grandson had children of his own.

But still they couldn't see the sun.

"We must work faster," said the grandson. "We have to reach the sun before my grandfather dies."

So they built the greatest machine ever made. With wheels as tall as houses, it could cross the world and lift entire buildings in its mighty arms.

From every continent they took fabulous buildings and piled them up, higher and higher.

Then, at last, the sky grew lighter.

EX LOCATION: PISA
BUILDING: tower
TYPE | leaning
QUANTITY: one

The old man, who had once been the richest man in the world, sat at the top of the tower holding his great-grandson in his ancient arms. He felt the warmth of life shine on his skin as it had done in his youth, and in the evening they carried him down to bed.

Every day after that,
an endless line of people climbed
the tower until every man, woman, and
child on earth had seen the sun. One by one,
they gazed in silence at the light that had given
them life. And as the Great Wall of China had been to
generations before, the Great Tower would stand as their memorial.